Whirlwind

by

Judith O'Neill

Illustrated by Pam Smy

For Hannah and Laurie, Emily and
Miriam, with love

First published in Great Britain by Barrington Stoke Ltd
10 Belford Terrace, Edinburgh, EH4 3DQ
Copyright © 1999 Judith O'Neill
Illustrations © Pam Smy
The moral right of the author has been asserted in
accordance with the Copyright, Designs and
Patents Act 1988
ISBN 1-902260-34-1
Printed by Polestar AUP Aberdeen Ltd

MEET THE AUTHOR - JUDITH O'NEILL

What is your favourite animal?
Kangaroo
What is your favourite boy's name?
John
What is your favourite girl's name?
Isabella
What is your favourite food?
Apple pie and cream
What is your favourite music?
Schubert's *Winterreise*
What is your favourite hobby?
Camping in our little dome
tent and swimming in the sea,
even off Scotland

MEET THE ILLUSTRATOR - PAM SMY

What is your favourite animal?
A cat called Buster
What is your favourite boy's name?
Jake
What is your favourite girl's name?
Daisy
What is your favourite food?
Indian vegetarian
What is your favourite music?
Blondie and Van Morrison
What is your favourite hobby?
Lying on the sofa reading
travel books

Barrington Stoke was a famous and much-loved story-teller. He travelled from village to village carrying a lantern to light his way. He arrived as it grew dark and when the young boys and girls of the village saw the glow of his lantern, they hurried to the central meeting place. They were full of excitement and expectation, for his stories were always wonderful.

Then Barrington Stoke set down his lantern. In the flickering light the listeners were enthralled by his tales of adventure, horror and mystery. He knew exactly what they liked best and he loved telling a good story. And another. And then another. When the lantern burned low and dawn was nearly breaking, he slipped away. He was gone by morning, only to appear the next day in some other village to tell the next story.

Contents

Chapter 1
The Old Road

"I think we'll take the old road home," Dad said as they drove away from Uncle Harry's farm.

"That road's very steep, dear," Mum said. "And very rough, too. Hardly anyone uses it these days."

"And it twists round and round like a corkscrew!" Tim shouted at the top of his voice, as he bounced up and down noisily on the back seat. "I love it! I love it!"

Tim's red hair was untidy and his eyes were very blue. He was nine years old. His sister, Jeanie, was twelve.

Jeanie said nothing. She hated that old road over the mountains. It seemed to hang halfway up the steep slope. She was scared of the deep drop to the gully on one side but she didn't want anyone to know she was scared. So she just hummed a quiet tune as if she didn't care at all. She took the green ribbon off the end of her long, thick hair. She made sure that the rubber band was firmly in place. She tied the ribbon again in a large, floppy bow.

"Couldn't we take the highway instead?" Mum asked. "We'd be home much sooner."

Jeanie hoped and hoped that Dad would say, *Yes!*

"No, no!" Dad said to Mum, smiling at her. "Everyone goes on that smooth, new highway. It's far too boring for me! Let's just keep to this lovely, quiet road. When I was a boy we used to call it the 'bush-road'. I know all its twists and

turns off by heart. We'll take the old road. Everything will be fine."

Soon the car was climbing higher and higher between the trees. Jeanie didn't look out of the window on her right. She didn't want to see that terrible drop to the gully below. She stared straight ahead, over Mum's shoulder, at the bumpy, winding road. It wasn't even a proper road. It was only a dusty track.

The car lurched and bumped on the deep ruts. The engine's sound rose even higher until Jeanie thought it sounded like a scream. Mum seemed strangely anxious now. She was twisting her hands together as they rounded each new bend, but Dad was enjoying himself. He sang happily in his loudest voice.

The day was hot and dry and windy. Just the kind of summer weather you'd expect in January in south-east Australia.

"I can smell smoke," Jeanie said suddenly. She was always the best in the family at smelling things.

"Don't worry, Jeanie," Dad said to her, turning his head for a second to give her a comforting smile. "There's always a small bush-fire or two in the mountains at this time of year. Uncle Harry says there's nothing to worry about. Those fires are well to the north of us. We're going south."

Jeanie didn't like that hot, dry wind. It seemed to be blowing stronger every minute. The car rocked on its tyres. Dad gripped the steering wheel more firmly but he was still singing.

As they swung around the next sharp bend in the road, Dad stopped singing and gasped in surprise. They all gasped. Dad pressed hard on his brake. The car slithered to a stop.

"Kangaroos!" Tim shouted excitedly. "Look! A huge mob of kangaroos!"

"I've never seen so many at once," Mum said in astonishment. "And whatever is the matter with them all? They're leaping over the road and down into that gully as if something were chasing after them."

"There's nothing chasing them, dear," Dad said. "They are probably smelling the smoke that Jeanie can smell. Those kangaroos want to get right down to the river at the bottom of the gully. They know they'll be safe in the water."

"I wish *we* were in the river at the bottom of the gully," Jeanie said gloomily.

Dad just laughed. Now the kangaroos had plunged out of sight. The old road was empty again. Dad turned on his engine.

"We're nearly at the top of the mountain, Jeanie," he said. "Soon we'll be going down the other side. You'll feel much better then."

On the other side of the mountain the wind was just as strong and the sky seemed strangely darker. The road twisted downhill, first one way and then the other way. Jeanie didn't feel much better at all.

"Perhaps there's rain coming," Tim said hopefully.

"Rain? In the middle of summer? I don't think so, son," Dad said with a laugh.

Dad drove much more slowly now. He kept close to the high, red cliff on his left-hand side and well away from the steep gully on his right. He leant forward in his seat and peered through the front windscreen. Jeanie could not see even one scrap of blue in the sky overhead. All she could see was a thick, black cloud that seemed to blot out the sun. She didn't like it. The car trembled and shook in the wind.

"Perhaps we could stop for a while, dear," Mum suggested.

To everyone's surprise, Dad agreed at once.

"What a good idea!" he said.

Tim thought Dad sounded rather glad to be having a rest. Tim himself was certainly glad. This journey wasn't nearly as much fun as he'd thought it would be. The corkscrew road had even made him feel a bit sick.

"I'll pull over to the tall cliff," Dad said. "That will give us some shelter. And we could have our picnic here in the car, couldn't we? Then when this wind has blown itself out, we'll all drive merrily home."

Mum was much more cheerful now. She unpacked the delicious picnic that Auntie

Marge had made for them – cheese sandwiches, apple cakes, hot tea in a flask and a bag full of oranges. Jeanie wolfed down the food.

"Chew carefully, dear," Mum said. "You're eating far too fast."

"I know I am," Jeanie admitted. "But I don't know why."

"You're scared!" Tim sneered. He was laughing at her.

"Yes," Jeanie said. "I am a bit scared. I don't mind the wind so much. It's this darkness in the middle of a summer's day that scares me. Aren't you three scared too?"

No one answered her. The wind howled as it pushed against the car with all its strength.

The car shuddered but its wheels stayed firmly on the ground.

"Let's sing some songs while we wait," Mum said. She tried to sound bright and happy but her voice was shaking.

"Mum," Tim said seriously, "I don't really feel like singing any songs."

"Neither do I!" Jeanie agreed.

So the four of them sat in silence, eating their picnic and waiting for the dry wind to pass.

Chapter 2
Into the Whirlwind

Everyone felt much better after that picnic.
The wind was still blowing hard but the sky
was not quite so dark.

"Let's be off," Dad said briskly. "I want to get
you all safely home as soon as I can."

He drove very slowly, still keeping close to
the red cliff on their left. The car crept down the
twisting road as slowly as a snail.

"Listen!" Jeanie said suddenly, sitting bolt upright in surprise.

"I can only hear the wind," Mum said, turning her head this way and that.

"The birds!" Jeanie shouted. "Look! There they go!"

A flock of red and green birds flew overhead. All of them were screeching.

"King parrots," Dad said. "That's what they are."

"Whatever's the matter with them?" Tim asked in amazement.

"They're scared!" Jeanie said.

"But why?" Tim asked her.

Jeanie just shook her head. She had no idea why the birds were scared. Then, just as the car turned around the next sharp bend in the road, Tim gave a wild shriek.

"Stop, Dad! Stop!"

Dad stopped at once.

"What's the matter, Tim?" Mum asked him.

Tim had undone his seat belt. He was standing up. He was calmer now.

"Can't you see it?" he said. His voice was very quiet. "Look straight ahead of you!"

They looked straight ahead. Then they all saw it. A huge pillar of red dust was whirling up from the road. It was just a little way in front of them. As they watched, the pillar of dust spun round and round. The top of the pillar climbed higher and higher. It seemed to touch the sky. And, worst of all, the pillar of dust was moving steadily along the road towards them.

"Whatever is it?" Jeanie gasped.

"A whirlwind!" Mum and Dad said together.

"The aborigines call it a Willi-Willi," Mum whispered as if she did not like to speak out loud. "I've never seen one before. But I've seen photos of them. I'm sure that's what it is."

Dad nodded.

"A whirlwind," he said. Dad always liked to know the right names for things. Tim sat down again.

"What will we do?" he asked.

"Sit still and stay in the car," Dad answered.

"No! No!" Mum said quickly. "That whirlwind could easily lift up the whole car and dump us over the edge of the gully. We should all get out and lie against the cliff. If we keep close to the ground, the whirlwind will soon pass over us."

"How do you know, Mum?" Tim demanded. "You've never even seen one before."

"I've read about them in a book, Tim," Mum replied. "*Lie flat on the ground*, the book said, *and keep your head down*."

"Right," Jeanie said. "I'm getting out! I feel trapped in this car."

"No, Jeanie!" Dad said firmly. "Just sit still! We're much safer in the car."

But Jeanie was out of the car already. Tim scrambled out behind her. Mum had her own door half open.

"Come back!" Dad called after them. Even *his* voice sounded scared now.

But Dad's warning was too late. The whirlwind had almost reached them. Jeanie and Tim had no chance of running to the shelter of the tall, red cliff at the side of the road. They flung themselves flat on the hard ground and lay still.

Suddenly the whirlwind was right on top of them. It roared and whined like a wild animal. The sun was blotted out. Dust and dry leaves were whipped against their bare arms and legs. They could hardly breathe. The gritty, red dust was in their hair, their eyes, their mouths.

"Help!" Jeanie shouted but her voice was drowned by the terrible howl of the wind. She closed her eyes and pressed her cheek against the earth. She lay completely still.

A minute later, or ten minutes later, or half an hour later, Tim pulled gently on her arm.

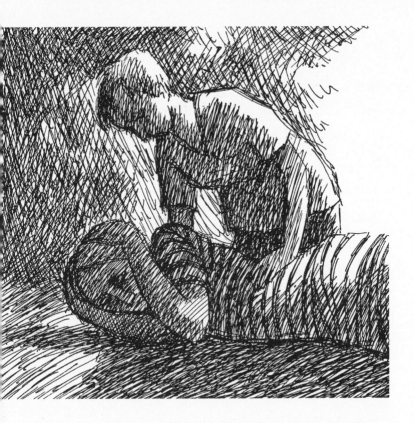

"Jeanie! Jeanie!" he whispered. "Please wake up!"

"I'm not asleep," Jeanie said, turning her face to look at him. "I'm just waiting for the whirlwind to go away."

"It's gone!" Tim said in his normal voice.

Jeanie sat up and looked around her. Tim was right. There was no wind at all. There was no dry dust. There were no whirling leaves. There was no smell of distant smoke. There was only the wonderfully fresh smell of rain. Jeanie's cotton dress was soaked. Tim's shirt was dripping wet. Rain was falling steadily onto the old red road and turning its deep ruts into slippery mud.

"Where's the car, Tim?" she said suddenly.

"And where are Mum and Dad?" Tim gasped.

Jeanie and Tim leapt to their feet and ran up and down the muddy road, calling and calling. There was no sign of car or mother or father or anyone else.

"They must have turned the car and gone back over the mountain," Tim said, standing still at last. "Back the way we'd just come."

"But why?" Jeanie asked him.

"I suppose they couldn't find us here. We were lost in that whirlwind. It scooped us up and hid us. So they must have thought we'd gone back to Uncle's farm. They decided to follow us."

"I'm not quite sure," Jeanie said. "The road's so narrow. Let's see if we can find any marks of the tyres where they turned the car."

Tim laughed.

"This rain will have washed away any marks by now," he said.

"I still want to look," Jeanie said firmly.

The two of them walked slowly back along the old red road towards the top of the hill, the way they had come in the car. They slipped in puddles and slid on the oozy mud.

"Look!" Jeanie cried in triumph at last. She was pointing to a clear line of tyre marks near the very edge of the road. "Some car has turned around here."

Tim stared at the marks.

"We can't be certain, Jeanie," he said. "Those marks might have been there for months."

"They look fresh and new to me," Jeanie said. "And now the rain is starting to wash them away."

"You might be right," Tim said at last.

"Of course I'm right," Jeanie said with a smile.

Suddenly Tim grabbed her hand.

"Jeanie! Look!" he gasped, pointing down into the deep gully by the side of the road.

At first Jeanie saw nothing but the blue-green forest. Then she saw two friendly eyes

peering out at her from behind a wet and
dripping tree. Around the eyes she saw a grey,
furry face. The face of a tall kangaroo. The
animal moved its head quickly to one side and
back again. Then it disappeared down the steep
side of the gully.

"He jerked his head," Tim said in excitement. "Didn't you see, Jeanie? He wants us to follow him."

"It's not a he, it's a she!" Jeanie said, laughing at Tim. "Didn't you see her pouch? Anyway, that jerk of her head means nothing at all. We can't possibly follow her down there!"

"Let's just look over the edge, Jeanie!" Tim begged her.

They peered over the edge of the road. All they could see were trees and still more trees growing right down the steep gully to the river far below. The rain kept on falling.

Jeanie pulled back in fear but Tim was already sliding one of his legs down the slope.

"Jeanie, we can easily go down here if we're careful," he said. "Look! The kangaroo is hopping between the trees. Let's follow her!

That's what she wants us to do. I'm sure of it!
She jerked her head again."

Jeanie never knew what made her agree to
such a crazy plan, but something seemed to be
pulling her over the edge of the gully.
Something seemed to be placing her feet
carefully one after the other but she had the
sense not to rush head-first to the bottom.

She moved in a slow, zig-zag path that
would lead them gently down to the river. She
grabbed first at one tree trunk and then at the
next to keep herself from falling. Tim was
always close beside her. His fingers clutched at
tufts of dry grass as he slipped and staggered
this way and that.

Far below them, they could still catch
glimpses of the bounding kangaroo. She really
did seem to be looking back over her shoulder
every now and then. She really did seem to be
making quite sure that they were following her.

Chapter 3
Down by the River

"This is more like a little creek than a big river," Tim said as they reached the dancing water at last. "Look at the way it swirls around the stones."

"It seems to sing!" Jeanie said in surprise. She loved the tree-ferns that grew so close to the creek.

"But where's that kangaroo?" Tim asked her, turning his head to look around him.

"She's gone!" Jeanie said. Her voice was flat with disappointment. "She made us come right down here just for nothing. How will we ever climb up to the road again?"

"Wait a minute!" Tim whispered in excitement. "I can see something! Look! Lying on the grass. Just by the water's edge."

Jeanie stared. All she could see was a wet, furry bundle on the ground.

"What is it?" she asked.

"Let's go closer and have a proper look," Tim suggested. He began to move softly towards the bundle. He thought the bundle seemed to shiver.

"It's a baby kangaroo!" Jeanie exclaimed in surprise. "A joey! Look at its tiny eyes watching us all the time! Look at its twitching ears!"

"But what's it doing here?" Tim asked her. "It should be safe inside its mother's pouch, not lying all alone on the grass in the rain."

"Listen!" Jeanie said, creeping closer to the joey.

Tim listened. Then he could hear it. The joey was making a soft, whimpering sound.

"He's crying!" Tim gasped in amazement.

"But why?" Jeanie said. "What's the matter with him? Why doesn't he just jump into his mother's pouch?"

"I think he's hurt," Tim said. "Let's have a proper look at him."

They squatted down beside the joey on the grass. They were careful not to touch him. They just looked. First at his wet fur. Then at his head and shoulders. Then at his floppy front legs. Then at his strong back legs.

"That's it!" Jeanie said at last.

"What?" Tim asked, bending his head still nearer to the baby kangaroo.

"See! There on his back foot, Tim! That deep cut. It's bleeding! I think he's hurt himself somehow and now he can't leap along properly. So he just lies there, panting and shivering."

"We'll have to help him," Tim said. "That's why the mother wanted us to come down here."

"Tim, you're imagining all that about the mother!" Jeanie laughed. "But you're right, we must try to help him. We could wash the cut first. That's what Mum would say, isn't it?"

Tim nodded.

Jeanie pulled a clean handkerchief from her pocket. It was wet already from the heavy rain but she dipped it in the river to make it wetter still. Gently she wiped the joey's bleeding foot clean. She dipped the handkerchief back in the water again and again. The joey was trembling. He looked at Jeanie with fear in his eyes.

"We'll need to tie something tight around the cut," Jeanie said. "Some kind of bandage. That would stop the bleeding and keep the sore foot off the ground."

"You could use your hair-ribbon," Tim suggested.

"Brilliant!" Jeanie said with a laugh of surprise.

She pulled the green ribbon from her hair.

She folded the wet handkerchief into a soft pad and pressed it against the joey's bleeding foot. Carefully she wound the green ribbon around and around his foot to keep the handkerchief in place. Then she took the two ends of the ribbon and tied a firm knot and a bow.

"There!" she said in triumph. "That looks fine!"

*****

The joey stood up slowly. He wobbled. He began to hop gently over the grass. He looked everywhere for his mother, turning his shy little face from side to side. The sore foot didn't seem to hurt him so much now.

Then he saw his mother behind a tree and he bounded towards her. He leapt straight into her pouch and snuggled down inside, leaving only his bandaged foot and his furry head peeping out. The mother kangaroo stood completely still. She was gazing in surprise at Jeanie and Tim.

Jeanie couldn't help laughing.

"The little joey looks so funny with that ribbon on his foot," she said. "Do you think we should try to push his foot right back into the pouch?"

Tim shook his head.

"Best to leave it alone, Jeanie," he said. "The joey seems to want it that way. We shouldn't touch him any more. And anyway, we must keep well away from his mother. She could give us a terrible kick!"

Jeanie backed off from the big, grey kangaroo as fast as she could.

"Let's climb up to the road again, Tim," she said quickly. "Mum and Dad must be frantic, wondering where we are. They'll think we're lost."

"We're not lost!" Tim said with a smile. "Mum and Dad are the ones who are lost!"

The long, slow climb up the side of the gully was much more difficult than the way down had been. Jeanie and Tim slipped about on the red mud until it was smeared all over their hands, their legs, and even their faces. The thick grass and bracken cut their fingers. Their bare knees bumped against rough stones. When they looked down into the gully below, they felt giddy. When they looked up they could see nothing but green trees and falling rain. Jeanie sneezed. Tim shivered.

"I wish I were at home in bed," he said in a small voice.

"So do I!" Jeanie said. She stopped and sneezed again. Then she grasped another tuft of grass in her hands and pulled herself higher up.

At last they were almost at the road. Then with one last heave, they were over the edge. They lay there, so tired that they could not move or speak. The rain was still falling.

Carefully, Jeanie lifted her head and looked along the road, first one way and then the other. She could hardly see anything at all through the thick curtain of rain, but she saw just enough to be sure that they were completely alone on the old bush road.

"Still no car!" she said with a sob in her voice. "No Mum, no Dad, no one at all!"

"We're really, really lost!" Tim cried out loud with a terrible groan.

They crawled slowly across the road to the shelter of the high, red cliff. They lay still. They slept.

Chapter 4
After the Rain

When Jeanie woke again, the night had come. The rain had stopped. A huge, yellow moon shone down on her face. She stared in surprise at her mud-stained hands, her filthy dress, her scratched legs. Then she suddenly remembered that terrible climb up from the gully.

"Tim!" she whispered into the night. "Where are you?"

"I'm here," came a thick mumble from close behind her.

Jeanie rolled over and there was Tim, sitting on the road! He was just as filthy as she was. His red hair was thick with mud. She hugged him. She even kissed him. She was so very glad to see him.

"Stop it!" Tim said with a splutter of laughter as he pushed her away. "There's no need for kissing, Jeanie! What are we going to do?"

"We can't do much in the middle of the night," Jeanie said, staring at the shadowy trees in the dark. "We'll just have to wait till the sun comes up."

"That moon's so bright. I think we could start walking," Tim suggested.

"Which way?" Jeanie asked him.

"Back the way we came, of course, silly!" Tim said firmly. "We mustn't go any further onwards. We know they turned the car. So we have to go back towards Uncle's house."

"But they might have simply gone further on along this road," Jeanie said. "We can't be completely sure that they turned the car."

"I'm sure," Tim said.

Jeanie was silent. There was a puzzled look on her face. Tim could see her quite clearly in the moonlight.

"Well, if you don't want to walk, Jeanie, we could just wait here," Tim said. "Perhaps a car will come along. We could wave and shout at the people in the car. We could make them stop."

"I don't think any cars ever come along this road, Tim," Jeanie said sadly. "Not in the night, anyway. Most people use the highway. That's what Dad said."

"Then we'd better walk," Tim said. "Back the way we came!"

He stood up and pulled Jeanie to her feet.

"Come on," he said.

At that very moment Jeanie and Tim began to notice the night noises all around them. A heavy bird flew low over their heads. An owl perhaps? They could hear his wings. An unknown animal cried out loud in the distance. Leaves moved restlessly in the wind and rain, rustling and hissing.

There was a sudden scuttling sound very close to Jeanie's foot. She jumped in fear and the noise stopped at once.

"I love walking in the bush in the daytime, Tim," she said, "but I don't much like it at night."

"You know what Dad always says," Tim said with a cheerful laugh. "He told us that we're always safe in the bush if we keep to the track. Apart from snakes, of course. And I don't think snakes slither around at night. They're probably all fast asleep."

Jeanie shuddered.

"I wish I were fast asleep," she said.

They trudged on in silence for ten minutes.

"Listen!" Tim said suddenly.

"What is it?" Jeanie asked him,

"I think there's a car coming up the road behind us. I can hear that high noise of an engine. What should we do, Jeanie?"

"Shout and yell to make them stop," she answered at once. "They're going the same way as we are. Ask them to take us to the nearest town. Tell them we're lost."

"But Dad says we're never to go with strangers," Tim said seriously. "Those people in the car that's coming up the road are sure to be strangers."

"I'd sooner go with a stranger than walk in the bush all night," Jeanie said.

"I wouldn't!" said Tim. "We mustn't stop this car, Jeanie. We mustn't let them see us at all. We'll hide at the side of the road till the car's gone past."

Jeanie was suddenly angry with Tim. She stood still in the middle of the road. "This might be our only chance!" she shouted at him. "You can do what you like, Tim, but I'm going to stop that car!"

"No!" Tim shouted back at her. "Remember what Dad always says to us! No strangers!"

In a blaze of white headlights, the car was now coming towards them. Its engine groaned. Tim ran to the shallow gutter at the side of the road and pressed his face against the red cliff. Jeanie leapt up and down, waving both her arms and bellowing out loud.

"Stop!" she cried. "Please stop!"

The car did not stop. Jeanie sprang backwards. She thought she could see two men crouched in the front seat and two women in the back seat but she was not quite sure.

She kept calling and waving as the car lumbered slowly past her and groaned its way up the red road. She even ran after the car for a little while but still it didn't stop. She turned back again.

"They didn't even see you!" Tim said. He had a grin of triumph on his face.

"They must have seen me!" Jeanie roared at him in fury.

"Perhaps they don't like to talk to strangers," said Tim with a laugh.

Jeanie burst into tears of rage. Then she stopped crying as quickly as she had begun.

"Tim!" she said to him in a cold, hard voice. "You can walk along this road all by yourself. You can trudge on for miles and miles in the dark. I don't care. I'm just going to sit here and wait for morning to come! Mum and Dad are sure to find us."

She marched to the tall, red cliff. She sat with her back against the cliff and her feet in the muddy gutter. She closed her eyes. She was still trembling.

Tim hesitated for a minute or two. He looked up and down the red road, wet and shining in the moonlight. He looked at Jeanie sitting against the cliff. At last he made up his mind. He walked quietly across the road and sat down beside her. Not too close, but close enough.

"Sorry," he said.

Chapter 5
The Way Back Home

When the red sun rose the next morning, the whole forest was alive with birdsong. Birds were calling, twittering, whistling and warbling. They were shrieking, grating and screeching. They were babbling, trilling and chinking. Yesterday's rain had left the forest damp and fresh. There was a scent of green leaves, and the rich scent of earth.

Jeanie woke up with a start. Tim was still fast asleep beside her, his head tilted back against the red cliff. She sat completely still and listened to the wonderful racket that the birds were making all around her. She had never been awake so early in all her life. She had never heard a dawn chorus as loud or as cheerful as this one.

Somewhere deep inside her, she felt a new flicker of hope. Perhaps today would be better than yesterday. Perhaps someone would find them. Perhaps someone would take them safely home to Mum and Dad. Or back to Uncle's farm.

"What's all that noise?" Tim asked, opening his eyes suddenly and looking at Jeanie.

"The birds!" Jeanie said. "They're just waking up. Like us."

"I'm hungry!" Tim said.

"Me too," Jeanie said. "But there's nothing to eat."

"Leaves?" Tim suggested. "Or berries? Or worms? Or beetles?"

Jeanie just laughed. She shook her head.

"There's sure to be another car coming soon," she said. "A car with kind people inside it. Not like those awful people who drove past us last night."

"Jeanie! I think I can hear it!" Tim said, jumping up suddenly in wild excitement.

Jeanie leapt to her feet. She listened. She could not hear a car but she could certainly hear something. A distant roaring sound was growing louder every minute.

"That's not a car, Tim," she said with a shiver.

"What is it then?" Tim said. "It's coming closer! Much closer!"

Jeanie grabbed Tim's hand and squeezed it hard. The bright morning sky was growing dark.

The top branches of the trees were lashing angrily from side to side.

"The wind!" Jeanie cried out loud in fear. "That terrible wind is coming back! Look, Tim, look!"

Tim looked down the mountain road. At first he saw nothing except the shaking trees but then he saw the dust. In the very centre of the road stood a tall pillar of red dust.

The pillar was whirling around and around. It was climbing higher and higher until it seemed to touch the sky. And worst of all, the pillar of dust was moving steadily along the road towards them.

"Another whirlwind!" Tim gasped.

"Or the *same* whirlwind," said Jeanie.

"What will we do?" Tim asked.

"Lie down flat and wait for it to pass," Jeanie said. "That's what we did last time."

"No!" Tim shouted. "I'm not going to lie down! That's not the best way. Let's walk right through the whirlwind, Jeanie, and out the other side."

"We could be blown over the edge," she warned him. "Down into that gully."

"You just hold tight to me, Jeanie," Tim said calmly, "and I'll hold tight to you. The whirlwind could never pick up two of us at once and throw us over the edge."

"I'm not so sure," Jeanie said. Her voice was shaking.

"Scaredy cat!" Tim laughed.

That scornful laugh made Jeanie change her mind in a flash. She grabbed Tim by the hand. She strode out boldly towards the whirling

illar of dust. She pulled him right into the heart
f the whirlwind.

A terrible roaring filled their ears. The dust
ricked their eyes and filled their mouths. The
wind tore at their cheeks and pulled at their
:lothes. They staggered. They almost fell. They
eant against the wind. They leant against each
ther.

"Keep moving forwards, Tim!" Jeanie houted. "Don't stand still!"

Tim pressed his body against the wind. lowly it began to open in front of him, like a eavy, wooden door.

"Push harder, Jeanie!" Tim shouted.

Jeanie pushed harder.

"We're nearly through!" she yelled.

In a sudden rush, the whirlwind lashed out t their legs and was gone. Jeanie and Tim tood in the centre of the red road. The roar of he wind grew fainter and fainter.

The dark cloud moved away from the sun's ace. The sun shone down on them, golden and varm.

"So there you are at last!" came a happy voice, close by their side. "You're walking out of the whirlwind!"

"Dad!" Jeanie and Tim shouted together.

"Jeanie! Tim!" came their mother's familiar voice, just as close.

"Mum!" Tim and Jeanie cried out in joy.

"We've been searching everywhere for an hour or more," said Mum. "We drove back towards the farm for a few miles, just to the top of the mountain. There was no sign of you so we thought we'd better come back here again. Wherever did you get to?"

When the hugging was over, Jeanie looked at Mum with puzzled eyes.

"Did you say you'd been searching for us for an hour or more?" she asked. "I'm sure we've been gone much, much longer than a couple of hours, Mum. We thought we were away all night. We saw the yellow moonlight. We saw the sun come up. We heard the birds singing their songs in the early morning."

Dad and Mum gazed at each other in amazement. Dad glanced at his watch.

"It's less than two hours, Jeanie. You must have been dreaming."

Jeanie looked at Tim. Tim looked back at Jeanie. They shook their heads.

"It wasn't a dream, Dad," Tim said firmly.

"Perhaps it was a time-slip or something strange like that," Mum said with a laugh. "Those whirlwinds can snatch you up and you never know where they'll put you down. I have heard of such things. But whatever it was, let's forget all about it now. We've found you safe and sound. That's all that matters. And we've

ot the most amazing thing to tell you. We saw a
angaroo by the side of the road. She let us come
p really close. She was a mother kangaroo with
 joey in her pouch."

"Yes!" Dad broke in. His voice was wildly
xcited. "The strangest thing of all was that
his joey had a green ribbon tied around one of
is back feet. The foot was sticking right out of
is mother's pouch in the funniest way. And
here was the green ribbon tied in a big floppy
ow."

"A green ribbon?" Jeanie asked, fiddling with
he end of her hair.

"Yes, dear," said Mum, still smiling. "Just
ike your own green ribbon, Jeanie. That one you
lways tie on your hair. By the way, dear, where
s your lovely, long, green ribbon?"

"Oh!" Jeanie said calmly. "I must have lost it
n the whirlwind. Sorry, Mum."

But as the four of them climbed into the car, Jeanie looked straight at Tim and Tim looked straight at Jeanie. Tim raised his eyebrows. Jeanie winked at Tim.

"So it wasn't a dream after all," Jeanie whispered into his ear.

Tim and Jeanie leant back in their seats. They smiled happily.

 Other Barrington Stoke titles available

What's Going On, Gus? by Jill Atkins 1-902260-10-4
Nicked! by David Belbin 1-902260-29-5
Bungee Hero by Julie Bertagna 1-902260-23-6
Hostage by Malorie Blackman 1-902260-12-0
The Two Jacks by Tony Bradman 1-902260-30-9
Starship Rescue by Theresa Breslin 1-902260-24-4
Ghost for Sale by Terry Deary 1-902260-14-7
Sam the Detective by Terrance Dicks 1-902260-19-8
Billy the Squid by Colin Dowland 1-902260-04-X
Eddie and the Zedlines by Colin Dowland 1-902260-31-
Kick Back by Vivian French 1-902260-02-3
The Gingerbread House by Adèle Geras 1-902260-03-
Danny's Great Goal by Michael Hardcastle 1-902260-32-5
Ship of Ghosts by Nigel Hinton 1-902260-33-3
Virtual Friend by Mary Hoffman 1-902260-00-7
The Genie by Mary Hooper 1-902260-20-1
Tod in Biker City by Anthony Masters 1-902260-15-5
Wartman by Michael Morpurgo 1-902260-05-8
Extra Time by Jenny Oldfield 1-902260-13-9
Screw Loose by Alison Prince 1-902260-01-5
Life Line by Rosie Rushton -902260-21-X
Problems with a Python by Jeremy Strong 1-902260-22-8
Lift Off by Hazel Townson 1-902260-11-2

Barrington Stoke, 10 Belford Terrace, Edinburgh EH4 3DQ
Tel: 0131 315 4933 Fax: 0131 315 4934
E-mail:info@barringtonstoke.co.uk
Website: www.barringtonstoke.co.uk